APPLESAUCE
IS FUN TO WEAR

by Nancy Raines Day   art by Jane Massey

cameron kids

Applesauce is fun to wear

on your nose

or in your hair.

Milk's delicious. Take a sip.
Make a mustache on your lip.

Toast is always nice and flat.

What could make a better hat?

Scrambled egg is good to smear
on your forehead
or your ear.

Mashed banana? Baby loves.

Try it on as gloppy gloves!

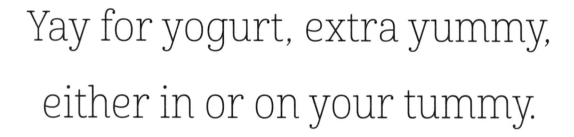

Yay for yogurt, extra yummy,

either in or on your tummy.

Black beans? Why not stick them on?

Make Mom think your teeth are gone!

Slurp up noodles of spaghetti.

Throw it in the air—confetti!

Roly-poly peas are fine

to squish

or fling

or put in line.

Ice cream—such a chilly treat.
Drip, drip, drip!
It cools your feet.

Birthday cake! Let's have a race.

Can you cover your whole face?

Head to toe, you are a mess!

Let's make you a bubble dress.

E DAY
Day, Nancy Raines,
Applesauce is fun to wear /

FOR JESSE, MALLORY, AND THE NEWEST DAY
—N.R.D.

FOR ARLENE AND NANCY xx
—J.M.

Book design by Melissa Nelson Greenberg

Library of Congress Cataloging-in-Publication Data available.
ISBN: 978-1-951836-05-4
Printed in China.

10 9 8 7 6 5 4 3 2 1

Cameron Kids is an imprint of Cameron + Company

Cameron + Company
Petaluma, California
www.cameronbooks.com